Samil Malice

in

The Great Flying Nappy Plot

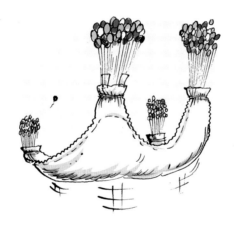

Written by Abie Longstaff • Illustrated by Sholto Walker

Turn to page 23 to read

Samil Malice

in

Wicked
Ice Cream Sunday

Published by Pearson Education Limited, Edinburgh Gate, Harlow, Essex, CM20 2JE
Registered company number: 872828

www.pearsonschools.co.uk

Text © Abie Longstaff 2011

Designed by Bigtop
Original illustrations © Pearson Education 2011
Illustrated by Sholto Walker

The right of Abie Longstaff to be identified as author of this work has been asserted
by her in accordance with the Copyright, Designs and Patents Act 1988.

First published 2011

15 14 13 12 11
10 9 8 7 6 5 4 3 2

British Library Cataloguing in Publication Data
A catalogue record for this book is available from the British Library

ISBN 978 1 408 27393 7

Printed and bound in Malaysia, CTP - PJB

Acknowledgements
We would like to thank the children and teachers of Bangor Central Integrated
Primary School, NI; Bishop Henderson C of E Primary School, Somerset;
Brookside Community Primary School, Somerset; Cheddington Combined School,
Buckinghamshire; Cofton Primary School, Birmingham; Dair House Independent
School, Buckinghamshire; Deal Parochial School, Kent; Newbold Riverside Primary
School, Rugby and Windmill Primary School, Oxford for their invaluable help in the
development and trialling of the Bug Club resources.

Every effort has been made to contact copyright holders of material reproduced in
this book. Any omissions will be rectified in subsequent printings if notice is given to
the publishers.

Samil Malice was walking home from school, looking forward to the weekend. Would he ...

play on the computer?

read comics?

go skateboarding?

No. He wouldn't do any of those things. For in the back garden, spread out on the lawn, was an enormous nappy. His father scampered around excitedly, attaching balloons to it. His mother scribbled mathematical equations on a blackboard.

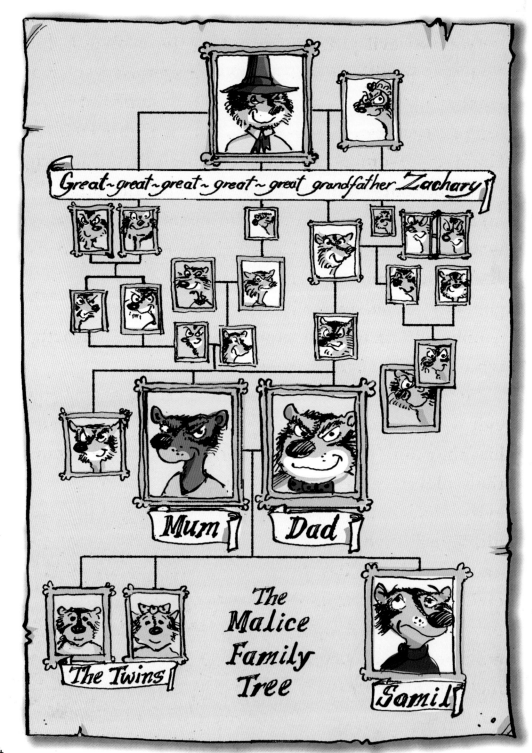

Great~great~great~great~great grandfather Zachary

Mum

Dad

The Twins

The Malice Family Tree

Samil

Another evil plot was afoot in the Malice house. You see, Samil's parents were evil geniuses ... or at least they *thought* they were. Samil came from a long line of evil raccoons that went right back to Great-great-great-great-great-grandfather Zachary, who had once tunnelled his way into the palace and accidentally come out in the guards' office, where he was caught and thrown in the dungeons. A few of Samil's ancestors really *were* evil geniuses ... but most, like poor Zachary, were simply not very good at being evil. This is exactly what Samil's parents were like.

Samil himself had absolutely no interest in being evil. In fact, he was really rather *good* – not that his mum and dad noticed. They just assumed that their oldest child enjoyed being evil as much they did. After all, Samil's baby brother and sister loved being evil. They were sitting on the lawn making milk-powder rocket fuel when Samil got home.

Samil looked at the giant nappy in the garden. "Dad, what's going on?" he asked.

Dad wasn't listening. "Ah, Number Three! Tie this balloon here, please!"

"Oh, Samil!" said Mum, her whiskers twitching in excitement. "Your father has another brilliant plan to overthrow the king."

"Thank you, Number Two," said Dad.

Mum swished her tail crossly. She hated being called Number Two. "I'm Number One," she growled.

The twins rolled on the ground laughing.

"Number ones, number twos!" they squeaked.

Dad gave a loud cough and stepped up onto a chair. Oh no! He was going to give one of his embarrassing speeches. Samil glanced over the fence to see if the neighbours were watching.

"This nappy we see before us is the first step in our plan to take over the kingdom. The world will finally see our genius! ... blah, blah ..."

Samil was too busy trying to shrink into the background to concentrate on the rest of the speech, but the plan basically went like this:

1. Make a giant nappy.
2. Float it up in the air using balloons.
3. Soak up all the rain that falls.
4. Hold the kingdom's rain to ransom until the king surrenders his power.
5. Take over the kingdom.

Wa ha ha!

"Great idea, eh, Samil?" said Mum. "Dad got it from the twins. Now they're potty-trained, we have all these spare nappies! We just sewed them together."

The twins filled their potties, then turned them upside down.

"And you're here for the great moment, Number Three! What do you think?" Dad looked at Samil, his big black eyes shining with hope.

What did Samil think? In truth, Samil thought that this plan, like every other plan his parents came up with, was utterly ridiculous. On a silliness scale of one to ten, the plan was a twenty-seven. This was, in fact, the stupidest plan he had ever heard. It couldn't possibly work ... could it?

But Samil loved his crazy family. So he just said, "It's brilliant, Dad," and Dad beamed as they watched the huge nappy floating majestically into the air. Samil had to admit, there was something rather magnificent about it.

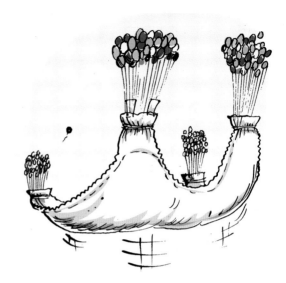

"Hooray!" Mum and Dad clapped their paws.

"Wa ha ha!" squeaked the twins evilly, fixing rockets to their pram.

At first, everything went to plan. The nappy absorbed all the rainwater. To everyone below, it just looked like a huge cloud.

Samil kept an eye on the newspaper headlines:

4th May
HUGE CLOUD, NO RAIN
Ducks organise protest march.

18th May
STILL NO RAIN
Umbrella shops closed for business.

8th June
KING'S GARDEN RUINED
Garden party may be cancelled.

And so it went on. For eight weeks there was no rain. The giant nappy grew fatter and fatter. Mum wrote a ransom note to the king. It read:

We have all your rain.
Surrender your power to us!
Wa ha ha!

Just as Mum's note was being delivered to the palace, something was happening high up in the sky.

A thirsty bird had discovered the nappy and was pecking a hole in the bottom. Water! The bird tweeted his friends and soon hundreds of birds were making thousands of holes in the nappy. The rain began to trickle down.

At that exact moment, the king opened Mum's note. He read it. He looked out of the window and saw the rain falling. He read the note again. He screwed it up and threw it away.

At the Malice house, Mum was in despair. "It's raining!" she cried. "All our work is ruined!"

"I'm sorry, Mum," said Samil. Although he was secretly relieved, he never liked to see his mother upset.

Neither did Dad. "Don't worry!" he cried. "I'll fix it!" He scampered out of the house with some more balloons. "Never fear, Number Two!"

"I'm Number *One*!" yelled Mum. "*You're* Number Two!"

"No, I'm Number One," said Dad, tying balloons to his paws and hind legs.

"I am!" replied Mum.

"No, I am!" said Dad, as he lifted off the ground.

"Be careful, dear," Mum called as Dad floated away, adding "and *I'm* Number One."

Dad waved his paws around crossly and the strings of the balloons became tangled.

Through binoculars Samil followed Dad's progress.

"He's reached the nappy!" Samil said. "But ... oh no!"

"What?" Mum cried.

"He's got caught in the strings!" said Samil.

Dad was now hanging upside down, waving his paws for help.

Samil had to save his dad. With the balloons all gone, he had to find something that could get him to the nappy fast. In the shed was the large catapult that Dad had built to bomb the palace with meatballs. Time to put it to *sensible* use.

Samil climbed into the catapult, pulled the lever and shot into the air. He flew so fast he was just a blur of black and white fur. Wham! He hit the soft, squidgy nappy.

"Samil, hurry! Untie me!" cried Dad as Samil slipped across the wet nappy. Quickly, Samil bit the balloon strings and Dad was free.

"Phew! That was close!" said Samil.

"Close," said Dad, "but exciting!"

Yes, thought Samil, *it was a bit.*

"Right, Number Three. Let's fix this nappy."

"No, Dad! We have to get down. This is dangerous," Samil said.

"Down? Oh yes ... but how?" wondered Dad.

"Let's just pop a few balloons," suggested Samil. He began popping and slowly the nappy started to descend.

Dad seemed sad at the thought of his giant nappy coming to earth, but as he looked over the edge his eyes suddenly brightened. "Brilliant idea, Number Three!" he exclaimed. "That's it, pop another one! Fantastic!"

Samil crawled to the edge of the nappy and peered down to see what his father was looking at. Oh no! So this was Dad's new plan.

Down below them was the palace. The garden was full of important animals and the king was just about to make a speech. An expression of amazement spread over the faces of the guests as, over the king's shoulder, they watched a giant nappy flying towards the palace. Faster and faster and closer and closer flew the nappy.

"Isn't this fun?" Dad danced as they hurtled towards the ground. "We're going to ruin the king's garden party!"

"Dad, sit down! We're about to crash!" Samil shouted in a panic.

The king was very pleased with the hushed silence of his audience, but as he turned round, he couldn't believe his eyes.

"Is that ..." said the king, pointing to the sky, "a great big flying nappy? It can't be!"

"Oh, yes it is!" cried the audience.

Splat!

The nappy landed on the roof of the palace tower and burst open. Rain water poured down the stone walls and drenched the guests.

"Guards!" cried the king. "We have a problem!"

"Wee?" sniggered the guards, looking up at the nappy. "Is that the Royal Wee?" They laughed so much that they didn't see Samil and Dad scampering down the tower.

19

Luckily, Mum had been watching through the binoculars and was now waiting at the bottom of the tower with the twins' rocket-powered pram.

Off shot the Malice family, tails flying in the wind as they made their escape.

Whooooosh!!!

Later that evening, there was celebration at the Malice house. Not for the Great Flying Nappy Plot, but for the ... er ... new Ruining the King's Garden Party Plot.

"We're evil geniuses!" cried Dad, jumping up and down on his back legs. "What a plot! What great raccoons we are! Well done, everyone!"

Samil shrugged. What could he do? At least there was rain in the kingdom again ... and he'd got to fly on a giant nappy!

"Well done, Dad," he sighed as Dad hugged him.

"Yes, well done, Number Two!" said Mum.

"I'm Number *One!*"

"Dear, I have *always* been Number One."

"Number ones, number twos!" the twins squeaked. Everyone laughed.

Samil Malice
in
Wicked
Ice Cream Sunday

Written by Abie Longstaff • Illustrated by Sholto Walker

One Sunday, Samil Malice was picking up his little brother and sister from a party. Nervously, he rang the doorbell. The twins weren't often invited to parties. Not twice, anyway. The door opened.

"Do ... do ... you know what they did?" shrieked Mrs Poodle, thrusting two small raccoons into Samil's arms. "They threw a rocket into the ice cream!"

Ah. The Malice family hated ice cream:
Ice cream was cold.
It got stuck in their claws.
And Great-great-grandfather Malice had nearly died falling into an ice cream vat ...
but that's another story.

"I'm so sorry," apologised Samil, but Mrs Poodle was too furious to listen.

"There's ice cream dripping from my ceiling!" she shouted.

Samil could still hear Mrs Poodle yelling as he dragged his brother and sister down the street.

"Did you make rockets again?" Samil asked.

"Wa ha ha!" the twins squeaked evilly. Samil sighed. Mum and Dad would be proud.

You see, Samil's parents were evil geniuses ... or at least they *thought* they were. Samil came from a long line of evil raccoons. His Great-great-great-aunt Matilda had once invented a flying machine so she could drop water bombs into the palace, but she took off in thick fog, lost her way and ended up in the Himalayas with not enough fuel to get back. A few of Samil's ancestors really *were* evil geniuses ... but most, like poor Matilda, were simply not very good at being evil. This is exactly what Samil's parents were like.

Weirdly, Samil had no interest in being evil. In fact, he was really rather *good.* Not that Mum and Dad noticed – they were far too busy plotting against the king. Even though Samil wasn't evil, he loved his parents, so he had no choice but to go along with their crazy schemes. Anyway, he wanted to be there to rescue them when they got into trouble.

Samil opened the front door and the twins rushed into the kitchen to make more rockets from the contents of their party bags. Samil followed to find Dad looking through a pair of binoculars.

"Look there, Number Two!" Dad said to Mum, his whiskers twitching in outrage. "That stuck-up badger king is having some kind of fair at the palace."

"I'm Number *One*," Mum growled and she snatched the binoculars from Dad. She hated being called Number Two.

"Oh no!" Mum shuddered, her fur standing on end. "It's the Ice Cream Festival!"

The Ice Cream Festival was the king's pride and joy. Everyone loved it ... except the Malices.

They hated ice cream:
Ice cream was cold.
It got stuck in their claws.
And great-great ...
Wait! You know about that, don't you?

"Urgh!" Mum shook her head.

"This gives me a wicked
idea!" said Dad.

"Oh no, Dad!" Samil
pleaded. "Let's just leave
the king alone!"

"Never! We are evil
geniuses! We must spoil
his every endeavour!"
Dad was off on one of his
rants. "We will melt the ice
cream and make that badger
look like a fool!"

The twins clapped and squeaked in excitement.

"YES!" cried Mum. "Brilliant, Number Two!"

Hmm. 'Brilliant' wasn't the word Samil would
have used. He would have said the plan was insane
or mad, or perhaps even utterly ridiculous.

"Shame it's not a hot day," sighed Mum, "or the sun would melt the ice cream all by itself."

"The sun!" barked Dad in excitement. "Number Two, you are an evil genius!"

"Thank you, Number Two," replied Mum, proudly.

Dad ran to the garden shed and came back triumphantly with a large sheet of shiny metal and an enormous magnifying glass.

"We are going to make a deflector!" Dad bounced up and down on his hind legs. "We will direct the sun's rays onto the ice cream and the festival will be ruined!"

Mum clapped her paws and the twins squeaked in excitement.

Uh-oh! Samil knew what was coming. Sure enough ...

"It's time for a family outing!" cried Dad.

Now, your family might go on outings to the park or the zoo or the beach. But not the Malices, oh no. Their family outings meant:

staking out the palace,

or tunnelling under the palace,

or breaking into the palace,

or ... well, you get the idea.

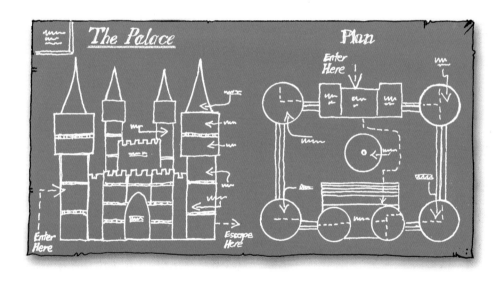

"Come on, Number Three," Mum cried, her tail swishing in excitement, "and bring the tool box!"

"Great, Mum," Samil sighed.

At the palace, a string quartet was gently playing music while the elegant guests tucked into their ice creams and chatted to each other. At the top of the garden steps stood a huge ice cream sculpture of the king riding a horse. The king stood next to it, doing his best to pretend that he knew how to ride a horse. Everything was very calm. Everything was very cool.

Meanwhile, the Malices pushed Samil's old go-kart full of equipment towards the palace. They climbed quietly up to the tower roof and began to fix the metal in place.

Soon it was set up perfectly. The enormous magnifying glass hung from the tower. The metal reflected the sun's rays onto the magnifying glass, focusing the heat straight onto the king's sculpture.

"Wa ha ha!" the Malices cried, as they scampered back down the tower and raced away down the hill.

At the palace, the ice cream slowly began to melt. At the top of the steps the sculpture of the king began to groan. Suddenly there was a massive …

... whoosh!

The sculpture dissolved into a huge ice cream river, frothing down the palace steps and drenching the guests in a waterfall of sticky milk.

All at once, the palace garden was in uproar. The teenage otters decided to take advantage of the giant ice cream waterslide and soon everyone had lined up to have a go.

"Yee-hah!" cried the otters. "We can do it backwards!" They zoomed off at top speed down the slide and ...

Crash!

... straight into the king. The badger flew into the air and landed ...

Splat!

... on his Royal bottom.

The king lay on his back in a puddle of milk, wriggling his legs like a beetle. Some of his Royal subjects thought he had invented a new dance craze and they loyally joined in. Then the king started making a strange noise: "Gu...gu...gu!"

Everyone looked at each other. Had the king gone mad?

"Gu...gu...guards!" he finally spluttered. "We have a problem!"

The Royal guards came running, armed with ... straws.

"Hooray!" cried the guests and everyone tucked in to drink the ice cream.

"Mmm! Delicious milkshake!" they said. "Hooray for the king!"

The sticky milk river floated on and on to the palace gates and poured down the hill, getting faster and faster as it flowed.

Near the bottom of the hill, the Malice family had stopped to celebrate their victory.

"We truly are geniuses!" exclaimed Dad, proudly swishing his tail.

"Er, Dad?" Samil had spotted something speeding down the hill.

"We are so clever!"

"Dad?"

"Nothing can stop us!"

"DAD!"

"Nothing!"

"DAD!"

Dad turned to see an enormous avalanche of ice cream thundering towards them.

"Eek!" Dad squeaked and the family froze in fear, but not Samil. He grabbed his go-kart.

"QUICK!" he shouted as the ice cream avalanche hit. "Jump!"

Samil grabbed his little brother and sister and the whole family leaped onto the go-kart. Samil caught his balance and stood tall and proud, his tail streaming out behind him like a sail as they surfed home on the icy river.

"Woo hoo!" Samil laughed.

"Wa ha ha!" squeaked the twins. In their paws they gripped a slingshot and their home-made missiles. They had spent all day constructing them from balloons and glitter. Oh, and some gunpowder they just happened to have hanging around.

Fire!

They fired a missile and it shot through the air.
Boom! It exploded over the palace throwing up ...
glitter. Just glitter. Glitter twinkling down towards
the melted ice cream.

"Fireworks!" cried the guests. "Fireworks for our
milkshake party! Three cheers for the king!"

At home, Dad was celebrating. "Hooray!" he cried. "The festival was ruined! We did it! I bet the king was really, really embarrassed! I bet his black and white face turned bright red!"

Everyone laughed.

"What a family!" cried Dad. "What great raccoons!" He put his arms round his three children. "You are so evil! Mum and I couldn't be more proud of you." Dad choked back tears.

"Um ..." What could Samil say? His crazy family might be evil, but hey, he loved them anyway. Besides, that go-kart ride was fun! Samil smiled and hugged his parents. "Well done, Dad," he said. "You really are an evil genius."

"Thanks, Number Three," said Dad. "Now, who wants to paint moustaches on Royal stamps?"

"Wa ha ha!" The twins were first in line.